This book was purchased for

_____

For Grandpa Ted, Grandma Joey,
Grandpa Fred and Grandma Donna
–AJH–

To all parents who enjoy reading
picture books with their children
–JST–

Rocking Chair Publishing
1694 Plateau Dr. SW
Grand Rapids, MI 49509-6512

ISBN 0-9659787-0-2
Text Copyright © 1997 Amy Jo Hoekzema
Illustrations copyright © 1997 Jeffery Scott Terpstra
All rights reserved. Published by Rocking Chair Publishing
Printed by Dickinson Press
Grand Rapids, MI USA
Library of Congress Catalog Card Number
97-92456

A STAR from the LEAST

by Amy Jo Hoekzema

Illustrated by Jeffery Scott Terpstra

Winter was coming
again to the forest,
and that meant
Christmas was not
far behind.
Every day there were
more clues to be found.
At first the air grew
cold and snow
began to fall.

The animals hurried
and scurried in every
direction, working hard
to finish the burrows
and nests that would keep them
warm on the very coldest days.
The insects and spiders curled up
inside leaves and under rocks
where they would
be cozy.

The squirrels that scampered
about the yard on Mr. Cooper's farm
could smell more than the
usual odors of the farm.
The scent of spicy pumpkin pie
and sweet sugared candies seeped
from the kitchen of the
old farm house.

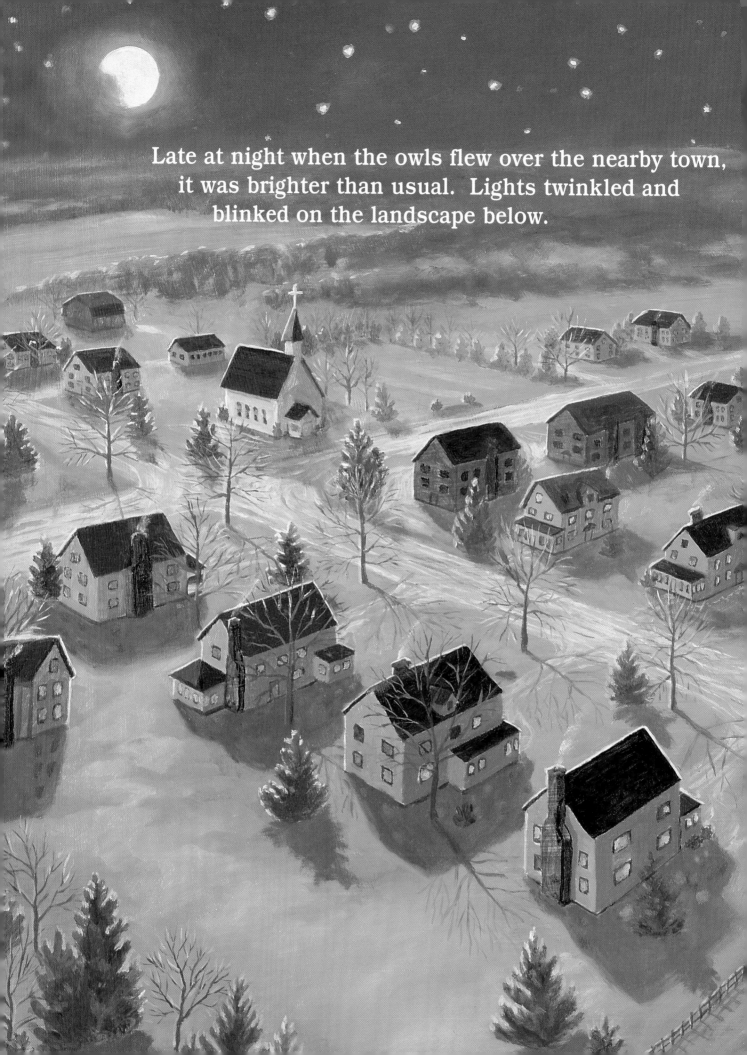

Late at night when the owls flew over the nearby town, it was brighter than usual. Lights twinkled and blinked on the landscape below.

As snow
began to pile up,
food became
more scarce, so the
birds flew to the farm
at the edge of the forest
to eat from the tray of seeds
and berries that Farmer Cooper
had set outside. While they sat
near the farmhouse window,
pecking busily at their food,
the birds could see the children
inside decorating an evergreen tree.
Another sign that Christmas was coming.

One cold afternoon,
the animals of the forest
gathered in a sunny clearing.
It was time once again to choose
a Christmas tree of their own.
"It's our turn to choose," chattered the
squirrels, "We know the most about trees."
"You don't know any more than we do,"
chirped the birds, "It's our turn to choose."
"We haven't had a turn in a long,
long time,"
said the
rabbits
with
wiggly
noses.

"Stop the racket," ordered the fox,
for he had the biggest voice.

"You know
the rules.
We must take turns.
Long ago the foxes chose
a tree. Then the turkeys
chose. The woodchucks,
skunks, rabbits, squirrels, birds,
and chipmunks each took a turn.
Now it is time to start
over again.
It is my turn
to choose."

Before the fox could hustle off into the forest, a spider lowered himself on a silky thread until he dangled at the tip of the fox' nose. "Excuse me, Mr. Fox," whispered the spider, "but the spiders have not ever had a turn. I believe we should choose the tree this year."

"Nonsense,"
chuckled the fox,
as he batted the spider
away with his paw,
"you are too small to
know how." The
animals all nodded their
heads in agreement.
So, without a second thought,
the fox trotted off into the
forest to look for a tree.

Before long, the fox
found a suitable
tree and all the animals
went to work.
The birds
got busy
dotting the tree
with cranberries
they found in the
tray at Cooper's farm.
Back and forth they flew,
gently carrying the red berries
in their beaks. The rabbits, skunks,
and woodchucks gathered pine cones, acorns
and soft green moss from the forest floor.
The turkeys gave instructions while the
squirrels and chipmunks scampered
up the tree with all the things
the others had collected.
They worked and worked
until everything was
just so.

It was late in the evening when all the animals
of the forest gathered around to view the tree.
"Done," said the fox.
"Finally," said the turkeys.
"Nice," said the woodchucks.
"Not bad," said the skunks.
"Pretty good," said the rabbits.
"We're tired," said the squirrels.
"Let's go to sleep," said the birds.
"Z - z - z - z," said the chipmunks,
for they were already asleep.
"It's missing something,"
whispered the spiders.

That night as the animals
of the forest slept, the spiders
went to work. Silently they crept
up to the top of the tree and
worked together throughout the
night to spin the most unusual
web they had ever created.

Just as they were putting on the finishing touches,
a few snowflakes fell from the sky.
Then the sun rose and sparkled
on the freshly fallen snow.
The Christmas tree shimmered
in the morning light.
The animals all awoke
to the most surprising sight.

"Magnificent," exclaimed the fox.

"Beautiful," exclaimed the turkeys.

"Radiant," exclaimed the skunks.

"Exquisite," exclaimed the rabbits.

"Splendid,"
exclaimed the birds.

"Delightful," exclaimed
the woodchucks.

"Dazzling,"
exclaimed
the squirrels.

"Gorgeous,"
exclaimed the
chipmunks.

The animals all stared at the tree and the
gleaming star at the top not knowing
what to say next.
At last the fox announced, "Next year the
spiders may choose the Christmas tree."
All the animals cheered in
agreement, but the spiders
didn't hear a thing...

...for they were already asleep.

To the Parent or Teacher

"Whoever receives this child in my name receives me, and whoever receives me receives him who sent me; for he who is least among you is the one who is great." Luke 9:48

The small spiders in this story represent not only the children of the world who often make enormous contributions simply by setting incredible examples of unswerving faith, lasting hope, and unconditional love; but also, all kingdom workers that, following Christ with childlike faith, work humbly behind the scenes to further His kingdom on earth.

It is our prayer that as you take time to teach your children about God, this story will serve as a springboard for discussions about dedicating their lives to the humble service of Jesus Christ.

Amy Jo Hoekzema

Jeffery Scott Terpstra

If you have enjoyed this book,

you may want to consider giving a copy as a gift.
To order additional copies contact:

Rocking Chair Publishing
1694 Plateau Dr. SW
Grand Rapids, MI 49509-6512

Phone (616) 249-9551